W9-BRM-726

# DK READERS

## Pre-level 1

Fishy Tales
Colorful Days
Garden Friends
Party Fun
In the Park
Farm Animals
Petting Zoo
Let's Make Music
Meet the Dinosaurs
Duck Pond Dip
My Dress-up Box
On the Move
Cuentos de Peces *en español*
Dias Ilenos de color *en español*

## Level 1

A Day at Greenhill Farm
Truck Trouble
Tale of a Tadpole
Surprise Puppy!
Duckling Days
A Day at Seagull Beach
Whatever the Weather
Busy Buzzy Bee
Big Machines
Wild Baby Animals
A Bed for the Winter
Born to be a Butterfly
Dinosaur's Day
Feeding Time
Diving Dolphin
Rockets and Spaceships
My Cat's Secret
First Day at Gymnastics
A Trip to the Zoo
I Can Swim!
A Trip to the Library
A Trip to the Doctor
A Trip to the Dentist
I Want To Be A Ballerina
Animal Hide and Seek
Submarines and Submersibles
Animals at Home
LEGO: Trouble at the Bridge
LEGO: Secret at Dolphin Bay
Star Wars: What is a Wookiee?
Star Wars: Ready, Set, Podrace!
A Day in the Life of a Builder
A Day in the Life of a Dancer
A Day in the Life of a Firefighter
A Day in the Life of a Teacher
A Day in the Life of a Musician
A Day in the Life of a Doctor
A Day in the Life of a Police Officer
A Day in the Life of a TV Reporter
Gigantes de Hierro *en español*
Crías del mundo animal *en español*

## Level 2

Dinosaur Dinners
Fire Fighter!
Bugs! Bugs! Bugs!
Slinky, Scaly Snakes!
Animal Hospital
The Little Ballerina
Munching, Crunching, Sniffing, and Snooping
The Secret Life of Trees
Winking, Blinking, Wiggling, and Waggling
Astronaut: Living in Space
Twisters!
Holiday! Celebration Days around the World
The Story of Pocahontas
Horse Show
Survivors: The Night the Titanic Sank
Eruption! The Story of Volcanoes
The Story of Columbus
Journey of a Humpback Whale
Amazing Buildings
Feathers, Flippers, and Feet
Outback Adventure: Australian Vacation
Sniffles, Sneezes, Hiccups, and Coughs
Ice Skating Stars
Let's Go Riding
I Want to Be a Gymnast
Starry Sky
Earth Smart: How to Take Care of the Environment
Water Everywhere
Telling Time
LEGO: Castle Under Attack
LEGO: Rocket Rescue
Star Wars: Journey Through Space
Star Wars: A Queen's Diary
MLB: A Batboy's Day
MLB: Let's Go to the Ballpark!
Spider-Man: Worst Enemies
Meet the X-Men
¡Insectos! *en español*
¡Bomberos! *en español*
La Historia de Pocahontas *en español*

# A Note to Parents

DK READERS is a compelling program for beginning readers, designed in conjunction with leading literacy experts, inclduing Dr. Linda Gambrell, Distinguished Professor of Education at Clemson University. Dr. Gambrell has served as President of the International Reading Association, National Reading Conference, and College Reading Association.

Beautiful illustrations and superb full-color photographs combine with engaging, easy-to-read stories to offer a fresh approach to each subject in the series. Each DK READER is guaranteed to capture a child's interest while developing his or her reading skills, general knowledge, and love of reading.

The five levels of DK READERS are aimed at different reading abilities, enabling you to choose the books that are exactly right for your child:

**Pre-level 1:** Learning to read
**Level 1:** Beginning to read
**Level 2:** Beginning to read alone
**Level 3:** Reading alone
**Level 4:** Proficient readers

The "normal" age at which a child begins to read can be anywhere from three to eight years old. Adult participation through the lower levels is very helpful for providing encouragement, discussing storylines, and sounding out unfamiliar words.

No matter which level you select, you can be sure that you are helping your child learn to read, then read to learn!

LONDON, NEW YORK, MUNICH,
MELBOURNE, AND DELHI

**For Dorling Kindersley**
**Editor** Vicki Taylor
**Designer** Jill Clark
**Managing Editor** Catherine Saunders
**Art Director** Lisa Lanzarini
**Publishing Manaer** Simon Beecroft
**Category Publisher** Alex Allan
**Production Editor** Siu Chan
**Production Controller** Nick Seston

**For Lucasfilm**
**Executive Editor** Jonathan W. Rinzler
**Art Director** Troy Alders
**Keeper of the Holocron** Leland Chee
**Director of Publishing** Carol Roeder

**Reading Consultant**
Linda B. Gambrell, Ph.D.

First American Edition, 2010
10 11 10 9 8 7 6 5 4 3 2 1
Published in the United States by DK Publishing
375 Hudson Street, New York, New York 10014

Copyright © 2010 Lucasfilm Ltd.™
Page Design copyright © Dorling Kindersley Limited

All rights reserved under International and Pan-American Copyright Conventions. No part of this publication may be reproduced, stored in a retrieval system, or transmitted in any form or by any means, electronic, mechanical, photocopying, recording, or otherwise, without the prior written permission of the copyright owner.

Published in Great Britain by Dorling Kindersley Limited.

DK books are available at special discounts when purchased in bulk for sales promotions, premiums, fundraising, or educational use.
For details, contact:
DK Publishing Special Markets, 375 Hudson Street, New York, New York 10014
SpecialSales@dk.com

A catalog record for this book is available from the Library of Congress.

ISBN: 978-0-7566-6313-1 (Paperback)
ISBN: 978-0-7566-6312-4 (Hardcover)

Color reproduction by Media Development Printing Ltd, UK.
Printed and bound in China by L Rex Printing Co., Ltd.

Discover more at

**www.dk.com**
**www.starwars.com**

DK READERS

STAR WARS

# Join the Rebels

Written by Catherine Saunders

DK Publishing

LUCAS BOOKS

My name is Luke Skywalker.
I live on Tatooine with my
Uncle Owen and Aunt Beru.

My uncle wants me to be a farmer but I would prefer to go to the Imperial Academy.

I want to be a pilot like my friend Biggs Darklighter.

**C-3PO and R2-D2**

Uncle Owen bought these droids from Jawa traders. C-3PO is a protocol droid. He can speak many languages. R2-D2 is an astromech droid.

My life is very quiet on Tatooine.
It is a remote desert planet.
Every day, I help my uncle on
his moisture farm.
But I dream of adventure!

**Death Star**

The Death Star is a huge space station. It is the Empire's most dangerous weapon. The Rebels are hoping to destroy it.

Life is much more exciting in other parts of the galaxy. It is also more dangerous. An evil Emperor rules the galaxy. He has built a powerful weapon that can destroy a whole planet. It is called the Death Star.

Some brave people have joined together to try and defeat the Emperor. They are called the Rebel Alliance. I would like to join them. The Emperor wants to destroy the Rebels but he does not know where to find them.

The Rebels have a secret base on Yavin 4. This is where they plan secret attacks on the Empire.

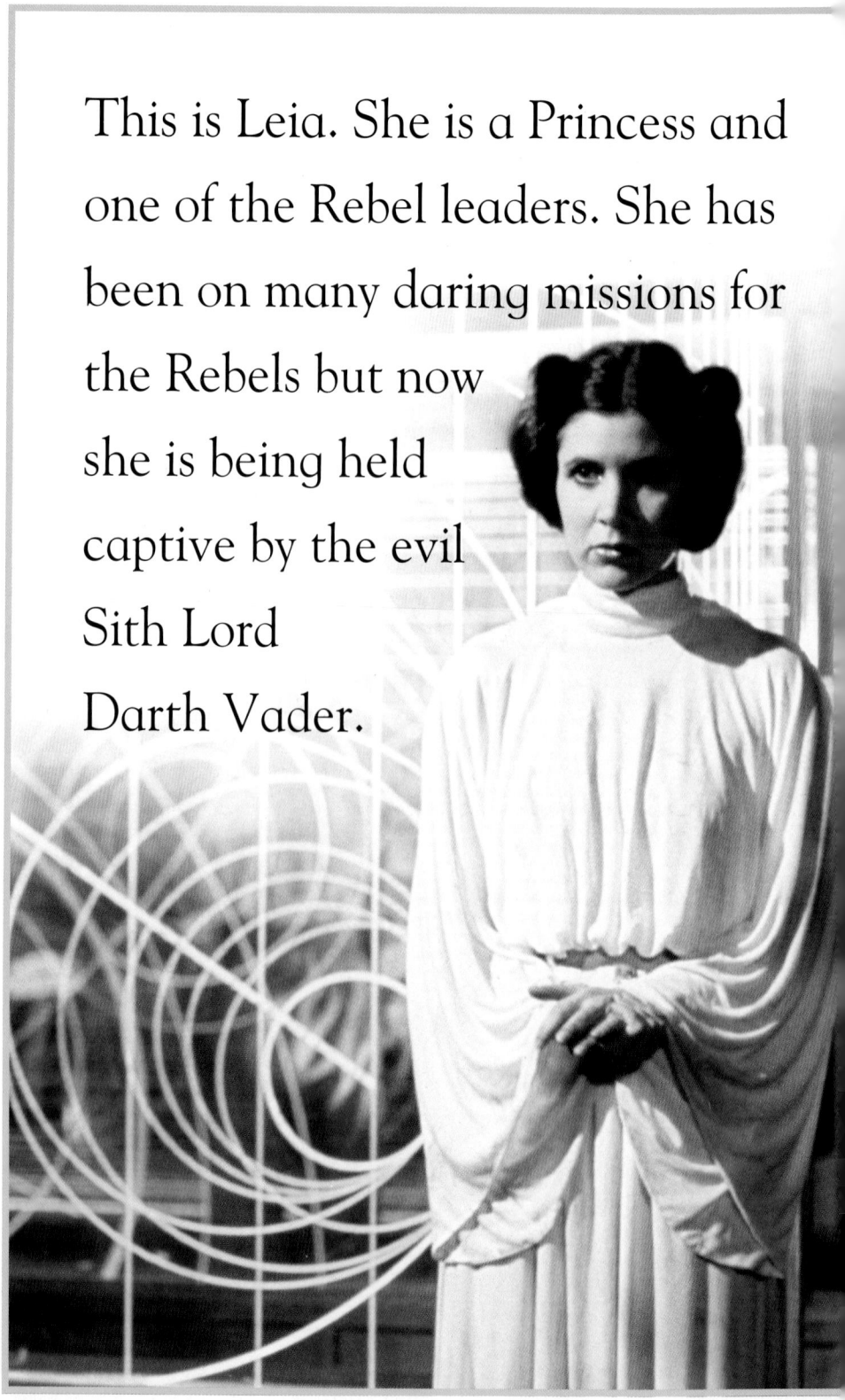

This is Leia. She is a Princess and one of the Rebel leaders. She has been on many daring missions for the Rebels but now she is being held captive by the evil Sith Lord Darth Vader.

My uncle's new droid R2-D2 has a message from Princess Leia. She needs help from Jedi Master Obi-Wan Kenobi.

I am going to help, too!

**Darth Vader**

Darth Vader was once a famous Jedi but now he serves the Emperor. He wants to crush the Rebel Alliance.

Princess Leia has hidden the blueprints of the Death Star inside R2-D2. Obi-Wan and I must take them to Princess Leia's home planet, Alderaan. We need to go there quickly! The *Millennium Falcon* will fly us there. It is one of the fastest ships in the galaxy.

Han Solo is its captain and a Wookiee named Chewbacca is his first mate.

The planet Alderaan has been destroyed by the Death Star! Now we are caught in a tractor beam and are being pulled toward the Death Star.

I am a long way from Tatooine and heading straight into a thrilling adventure.
I am determined to rescue Princess Leia and join the Rebel Alliance.

Being a Rebel hero is not easy. The Imperial stormtroopers are firing at us from all directions. Now we are trapped in a smelly garbage dump.

After many adventures, we escape from the Death Star and rejoin the Rebel Alliance. I am ready to help the Rebels fight back against the evil Empire.

Rebel pilots must be ready for action at all times. We are on a mission to destroy the Death Star. It is very dangerous but I am learning to use the Force.

**The Force**

The energy that surrounds all living things. Jedi knights use the power of the Force. Sith lords use the dark side of the force for evil.

I am flying a ship called an X-wing and the Imperial pilots are attacking us in TIE fighters. Many of my brave Rebel friends have already been lost. Luckily I have scored a direct hit and the Death Star is destroyed.

My first mission was a success.
The Rebels were triumphant
and everyone was so happy.
I felt like a hero.
Now I am learning that being a
Rebel is hard work. Imperial spies
are everywhere and we must
always be on the look out
for them.

The new Rebel base on Hoth is very cold.

The Imperial forces have discovered our new base! The stormtroopers have giant AT-AT walkers and are trying to destroy our power source.

The Rebels are ready for action and are not going to give up without a fight. I have a plan…

This battle is over and the Rebels must flee from Hoth.

We will live to fight another day.

The Battle of Hoth was a victory for the Empire but the Rebels are not beaten yet. We will overcome the Empire and free the galaxy. I am going to Dagobah to meet the famous Yoda and learn the ways of the Force. I will become a great Jedi warrior.

**Yoda**

Yoda may be small but he is a very powerful and wise Jedi. He senses that Luke has great powers and shows him how to use them.

The Force is showing me that my good friends Han Solo and Princess Leia are in danger.

Darth Vader has set a trap for them in Cloud City.
I need to rescue them.
I was right. Darth Vader is here.
I must fight him and help free my friends.

The Rebel Alliance is growing stronger. There is a new Death Star. We have a plan to destroy it and finally defeat the Empire.

**Moon of Endor**

Endor's forest moon is home to creatures called Ewoks. They may look cute but they are tough! The Ewoks help the Rebels to destroy the new Death Star.

The Death Star's shield generator is located on the moon of Endor. The Rebels are going to attack it!

The plan is working.
The shield generator is destroyed and the Rebel pilots are attacking the Imperial fleet.

It is time for me to face the Emperor himself. The Emperor is very powerful. But at the last moment, Darth Vader turns away from the dark side and defeats the Emperor. The Rebels have won and the galaxy is free at last.

# Glossary

**Blueprints**
Plans showing a map of where everything is on board.

**Daring**
Brave and adventurous.

**the Force**
The special power that both Jedi and Sith can learn to use.

**Imperial Academy**
This is where the Galactic Empire trains its army.

**Jawa**
The people who live on Tatooine.

**Remote**
A long way from anywhere else.

**Shield generator**
The machine that makes the protective shield around the Death Star.

**Sith Lord**
A high-ranking member of the Sith race.

**Tractor Beam**
A beam that can trace other ships and pull them in.

**Triumphant**
Happy, victorious, jubilant. Usually when you have won something, you would feel triumphant.

**Wookiee**
A hairy being that lives on the planet Kashyyyk.

# Index

Alderaan 12, 14
C-3PO 5
Chewbacca 13
Darth Vader 10-11, 27, 31
Death Star 7, 12, 14, 17, 18-19, 28-29
Empire 9, 17, 24, 28
the Emperor 7, 8
the Force 18, 24, 26
Han Solo 13, 26
Jedi 11, 24
*Millennium Falcon* 12
Princess Leia 10-11, 12, 15, 26
Obi-Wan 11
R2-D2 5, 11, 12
Rebel Alliance 8-9, 15, 17, 28
Yoda 24